For Olaf, with love
—Gaby Hansen

Text copyright ©2002 Jane Johnson
Illustrations copyright ©2002 Gaby Hansen

This edition published in 2007 by **tiger tales**,
an imprint of ME Media, LLC
202 Old Ridgefield Road, Wilton, CT 06897
exclusively for Hallmark Cards, Inc.
Visit us on the web at www.hallmark.com

First published in the United States 2002
Originally published in Great Britain 2002
By Little Tiger Press
An imprint of Magi Publications

Printed in China
ISBN 1-58925-347-7
BOK1098

3 5 7 9 10 8 6 4

Library of Congress Cataloging-in-Publication Data

Johnson, Jane, 1951-
   Are you ready for bed? / by Jane Johnson ; illustrated by Gaby Hansen.

      p. cm.
Previous ed. had title: Ready for bed.
Summary: Mrs. Rabbit has just put her children to bed and is ready to enjoy
the peace and quiet when Little Bunny announces that he cannot sleep.
   ISBN 1-58925-017-6
   [1. Bedtime—Fiction. 2. Rabbits—Fiction.] I. Hansen, Gaby, ill. II. Title.
   PZ7.J63216 Ar 2002
   [E]—dc21
                                        2002002780

Are You Ready for Bed?

by Jane Johnson

Illustrated by Gaby Hansen

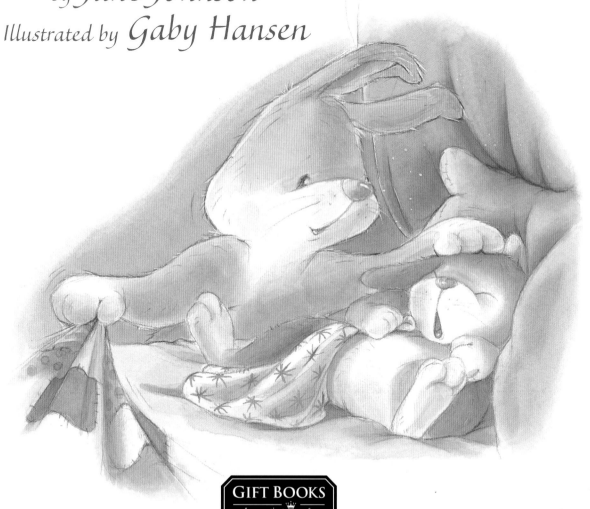

GIFT BOOKS
from Hallmark

tiger tales

Mrs. Rabbit sighed when all of her children were tucked safely into bed. "Ah, peace and quiet at last," she said.

But Mrs. Rabbit had spoken too soon.

"Mommy, I can't sleep," said her youngest child,
Little Bunny, interrupting her first snore.

Mrs. Rabbit tried a gentle lullaby.

"Hush-a-bye bunny on the tree top,

When the bough breaks, the cradle . . ."

Little Bunny's eyes began to close.

"Is my bunny sleepy now?" whispered Mrs. Rabbit,

so as not to wake the others.

"No!" said Little Bunny. "I'm not sleepy
at all." He wanted to stay up all night long
with his mommy.

Mrs. Rabbit tried a bubble bath.

"Rub-a-dub dub, my bunny needs a scrub," she laughed.

"Who's my Little Bunny?"

"I am!" Little Bunny said, smiling sweetly.

"Well now, darling, I think it's bedtime,"
Mrs. Rabbit said hopefully, drying his fur.

"No!" said Little Bunny. "It's not bedtime yet."

Mrs. Rabbit tried warm milk.

"Swirly, whirly, creamy white," she yawned.

"Time to cuddle and say 'Good night.'"

"Cuddle, yes! 'Good night,' no!" said
Little Bunny. He wanted stay up with
his mommy forever.

"Squeezy, huggy, snuggle up tight," he said happily. "Am I the best little bunny in the world tonight?"

"I love all my bunnies the same, sleepyhead," said Mrs. Rabbit.

"Then I'll never be ready for bed,"
said Little Bunny.

"What am I going to do with you?"
said his worn-out mother. Little Bunny
jumped up excitedly…

"Let's play bunny hops!"
said Little Bunny.

"Hoppity, hoppity, hop…

'round and 'round the
room till I…"

"Flop," whispered
Mrs. Rabbit.

"Zzz," snored
Little Bunny.

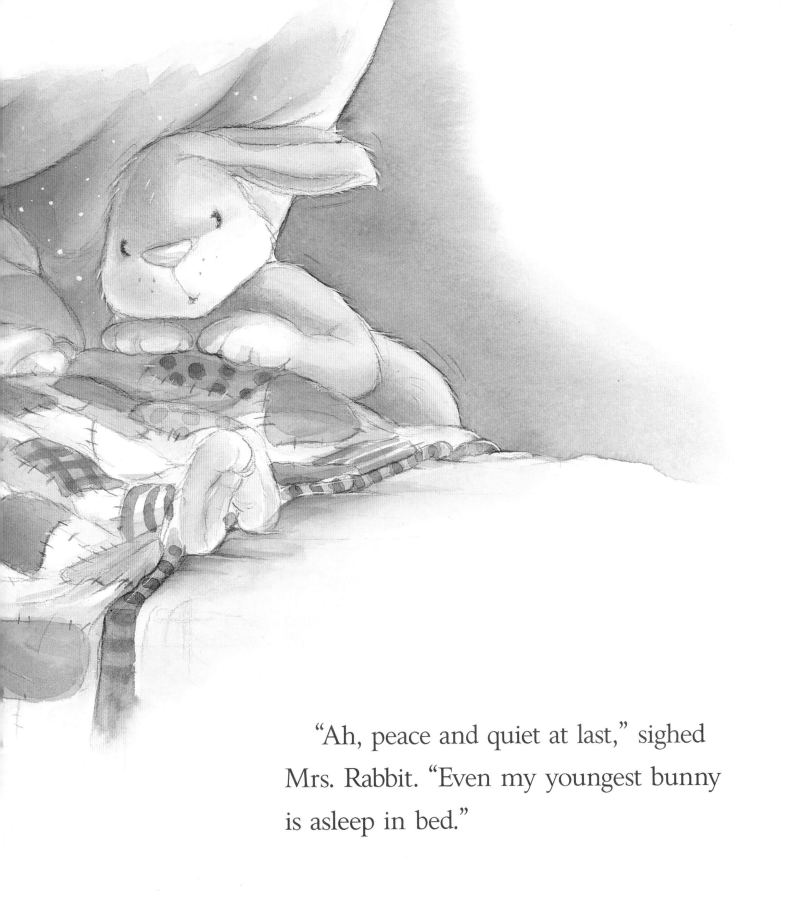

"Ah, peace and quiet at last," sighed
Mrs. Rabbit. "Even my youngest bunny
is asleep in bed."

Mrs. Rabbit flopped into
bed, but through her
snores she heard…

her second youngest bunny call out,
"Mommy, I can't sleep!"